The Moon Dragon

by Tony Abbott
Illustrated by David Merrell
Cover illustration by Tim Jessell

A
LITTLE APPLE
PAPERBACK

SCHOLASTIC INC.
New York Toronto London Auckland Sydney
Mexico City New Delhi Hong Kong Buenos Aires

For my little family

For more information about the continuing saga of Droon,
please visit Tony Abbott's website at
www.tonyabbottbooks.com

ISBN 0-439-67174-4

12 11 10 9 8 7 6 5 4 3 2 1   6 7 8 9 10 11/0

Printed in the U.S.A.
First printing, January 2006

Contents

One

Connections

"Come on, guys! We need to get up there fast!" shouted Eric Hinkle as he raced to the top of the Rainbow Stairs.

"Faster than fast," said his friend Julie Rubin, climbing swiftly after him. "If we don't, Droon won't be a secret anymore!"

"No kidding," added Neal Kroger. "Besides, our town isn't ready for dragons!"

"Or sorcerers!" said Princess Keeah, following right behind Neal.

The four friends were dashing up the shimmering, rainbow-colored staircase that connected the magical world of Droon with the Upper World — their world. Behind them were Keeah's parents, King Zello and Queen Relna; their trusty friend Max, an eight-legged spider troll; and Khan, the courageous pillow-shaped king of the purple lumpies.

They were all on a single mission: to find the boy sorcerer Sparr and the moon dragon Gethwing, who had escaped to the Upper World, and bring them back to Droon. If they didn't, the fates of both worlds were in serious trouble.

"Stay together!" yelled Julie as the friends entered a thick bank of clouds high in the Droon sky.

Climbing as quickly as he could, Eric couldn't help but think of the many strange connections between his world and Droon.

The pasts and futures of both worlds were closely entwined. And so were their people.

First of all, in the days when Lord Sparr did everything in his power to conquer Droon, a mysterious Sea Witch named Demither had brought the young Keeah to the Upper World. Together, they hid the magical Coiled Viper from Sparr.

Years later, Eric found the golden, crown-shaped Viper near his town library. To save the wizard Galen's life, Eric gave the Viper to Sparr. For the longest time, he wished that he had never done that. By giving Sparr such a powerful object, he felt as if he had helped the forces of evil.

But two amazing things had come of it.

The first was that when Sparr took the Viper, Galen gained possession of the Moon Medallion, a magical white stone made by his mother, Zara. The Moon Medallion held untold secrets about both worlds' strange pasts and mysterious futures. It was perhaps even more powerful than the Coiled Viper.

As he hurried up out of the clouds, Eric turned and saw the Medallion hanging now around Queen Relna's neck.

"I see the top!" cried Max, climbing next to Khan. "Just a little more —"

The second good thing to happen was that when Sparr used the Coiled Viper to wake the evil Emperor Ko from his long sleep, something went wrong with the charm and — *boom! flash!* — Sparr was transformed into a boy.

Lord Sparr had become Kid Sparr!

Now, as a boy, Sparr was helping them fight the fearsome Emperor Ko.

No one's more fearsome than Ko, thought Eric. *Except maybe for Ko's second-in-command, the moon dragon Gethwing.*

The gray-scaled, four-winged dragon was both ruthless and clever. Because an old legend proclaimed that "a boy would lead him," Gethwing had chased Sparr to the Upper World, convinced he would help Gethwing find another magical object hidden there.

The kids had to stop that from happening. No matter what.

"Here we are!" said Julie. She jumped past Eric into a small closet in the basement of the Hinkles' house.

Everyone piled in until the closet nearly burst. When Relna pulled the chain that hung from the bulb on the ceiling — *click!* — the light went on, the staircase vanished beneath their feet, and a gray cement floor appeared in its place.

"Oh, I love your world," whispered Khan. "I'm so excited —"

"And I'm so cramped!" said King Zello, hunching over. "Can someone check if it's clear out there? I'm ready to pop!"

Julie carefully turned the knob and opened the door. "Looks good to me —"

"Wait! My parents might be home," said Eric. He listened quietly.

Usually no time passed in the Upper World when the kids were in Droon. But after Sparr and Gethwing fled Droon, Ko had uttered a curse, and the magic stairs had disappeared for a while. No one knew how long Sparr and Gethwing had been in the Upper World, or what might have happened since the kids had been there last.

Finally, Eric smiled. "All clear. Let's go."

The eight of them squeezed out of the tiny closet and quietly climbed the basement stairs to the kitchen.

"I hope it's still the same Saturday we left," said Neal. "Because that means there's still no school!"

Eric smiled. "Maybe —"

Kkk! The twin horns on Zello's helmet

scraped the kitchen ceiling. "Oops," he said, pulling off his helmet. "Sorry."

When Queen Relna's silver crown flashed in the light from the kitchen window, Eric realized that their friends from Droon might need disguises. "I think —"

"You don't have to say it, Eric," said Keeah, smiling as she removed her golden crown. "If we're going out into your town, we need to blend in a little more."

"Girls, come with me," said Julie. "On Saturday, my parents always work in the backyard. We can sneak in the front and raid the closets. Guys, be back in a sec!"

While Julie, Keeah, and Relna ran across the street to Julie's house, the others headed upstairs. Rummaging through his closet, Eric handed Khan the largest, puffiest ski jacket he could find.

Max disguised himself in two sets of

football padding, an extra-large jersey, and a football helmet. Following Neal into Mr. Hinkle's closet, King Zello emerged a few minutes later nearly bursting out of a faded, flannel work shirt.

"That's my dad's lucky shirt!" said Eric.

"I know," said Neal. "We'll need luck to get away with this."

Before long, Julie, Keeah, and Relna were back, dressed like any modern mother and daughters. The two crowns and other royal finery were stuffed in Julie's bulging backpack.

"Okay," said Keeah. "Let's find Sparr."

"The Fifth River brought him and Gethwing here," said Eric, opening the back door. "It ends at the town pond. Let's start there."

"To the pond!" said Khan firmly.

Glancing both ways, the whole group

darted across Eric's backyard to the side street. They headed quickly past Neal's garage and down the next street.

"I hope Sparr's okay," said Julie as they turned left, then crossed two more blocks. "We've been through a lot together."

"Right," said Max. "Except that he and Gethwing have been through a lot, too. After all, it was the moon dragon who raised Sparr the first time around."

Eric was worried about that, too. He trusted Sparr now. The boy had saved his life more than once. It was Gethwing he didn't trust. The moon dragon had great powers. If he found Sparr, could he use those powers to turn him to the dark side again?

Eric stopped suddenly.

"What's the matter?" asked Zello, clutching his battle club.

"I don't know," Eric whispered. "But if it *is* Saturday, where is everyone? Why isn't anybody outside? There are no cars on the roads. I don't see anyone anywhere."

Max grumbled from under his helmet, "You mean I'm wearing this for nothing?"

"You may not need it *yet*, my spidery friend," said Khan. "But something's not right. Listen." The lumpy king tilted his head to the side. A moment later, everyone heard what he was listening to.

Stomp . . . stomp . . . It was the sound of slow steps dragging themselves one after another across the nearby street. Next came a terrible squeaking noise. *Errch! Errch!*

The little group looked around in every direction but saw no one.

"Uh, okay," said Neal. "I thought ghosts only came out at night."

Stomp . . . stomp . . . errch! The footsteps and the squeaking soon moved on, and the street was quiet once more.

Eric's heart began to pound wildly. He

looked back at his neighborhood, suddenly wondering where his parents were. "I don't like this. Time must have passed since we were here. Something's definitely going on."

The group listened for a while longer, but heard nothing else. They continued down two more streets before finding the path to the pond. When they arrived at the little beach, the small strip of sand was fully drenched in sun — but completely deserted.

"I don't like it at all," said Khan, frowning as he sniffed the air. "There is definitely something fishy happening in your town."

"Find out what you can," said Julie. "I think I'll take a Julie's-eye view."

"Be careful," said Relna. "Gethwing could be lurking anywhere."

Julie nodded. Ever since she had been scratched by an ancient creature called a wingwolf, Julie had gained the power to fly. Glancing around quickly to make sure no one was watching, she leaped into the air and soared up over the beach.

"It's very handy having our own personal Julie Bird," said Keeah.

As Julie flitted first to a tree, then over town to the library roof, Eric stared out across the pond. For the longest time, it was perfectly calm. All of a sudden, a head bobbed up from under the water. "Hey, everybody, look." Eric whispered. "Someone's out there!"

The head turned, glided for a short distance, then vanished under the surface.

"And they're spying on us!" said Neal.

When a small splash surfaced hundreds of feet from the first one, the shape was there again, still watching them.

Eric blinked. "Whoa. That was a long way to swim underwater!"

Suddenly — *blam!* — the air blazed with red light, they heard a scream, and Julie tumbled from the sky, fell into Khan, and rolled over in the sand.

"Yikes!" she cried, scrambling up. "The whole town is empty — except for them!"

Blam! Blam! The air flashed red again.

"It's Gethwing!" cried Relna. "Hide!"

In an instant, the terrifying moon dragon swept over the beach, his four black wings flapping noisily. Sparr was running across the sand, his black cloak flying, the small fins behind his ears glowing purple.

"Sparr, give it to me!" boomed Gethwing. "Give it to me now!"

"No way!" the boy yelled. "I wouldn't give you a stick of gum, even if I *knew* what you wanted! Go back to the Dark Lands! I'll light the way for you!"

"*We'll* light the way!" said Eric, joining Sparr. "Fire!"

The two boys joined their blasts and — *ka-blam!* — drove the dragon away, while Sparr fled the beach in a flash.

Gethwing hovered over the sand, glaring down at Eric. "You, you, always *you!*"

"Eric, run!" yelled Keeah, leaping to him.

But it was too late. Gethwing aimed a fiery bolt right at Eric. Before the boy could move — *wham!* — the air blazed red once more.

Two

Secrets, Memories, and Cakes

"Eric, watch out!" cried Keeah. She pushed him away just as the moon dragon's flame exploded on the beach where he had been standing.

"Enough!" boomed the dragon, soaring up over the street. "I'll deal with you later — I have more important things to do!"

"You won't follow Sparr!" yelled Relna. "Everyone — now!" Together, she, Keeah, and Eric hurled blue, violet, and silver sparks at Gethwing. *Ka-blam!*

The blasts struck Gethwing on the shoulder, and he fell heavily onto the sand.

"Ha! The bigger they are, the harder they fall," shouted Zello, twirling his club. "Everyone follow Sparr. Relna and I will keep this one busy!"

"Hurry, children," added Relna. "Find Sparr!"

"You heard the queen," cried Max.

Without delay, the children, Max, and Khan rushed down Main Street in the direction that Sparr had fled.

Before long, the sounds of Relna's sizzling blasts, Zello's whirling club, and Gethwing's howls receded behind them, and everything was quiet again.

Main Street was completely deserted.

"Where did Sparr go?" asked Max,

stopping and looking around. "He wasn't that far ahead of us!"

"It's Sparr, remember," said Julie. "He can probably vanish pretty easily."

"Everyone vanished," said Keeah. "Look."

The nearby coffee shop was empty, even though every table was covered with plates of food.

"Guys, we have a problem," said Eric.

"Yeah, but . . ." Neal put his hand on the coffee shop door. "Do you think they'll be back before the food gets cold?"

"Neal!" said Julie. "We're talking about our families, our parents. Everyone's gone!"

Neal dropped his hand. "I know, I know. I just hate to see food go to waste."

"Everyone, keep your eyes and ears open," said Keeah. "Khan, keep your nose open."

As leader of the lumpies, Khan was the

most talented of the danger-sniffing tribe of purple creatures. "I never leave home without it," he said with a sniff. "And right now, I smell something dangerous . . . just over there." He pointed down a side street. At the end stood a high-roofed building made of brick, with double doors in front.

"No kidding, something dangerous is going on in there," said Neal. "That's our school. It's where they keep all the math!"

"Maybe that's where Sparr is, too," said Keeah. "I think we need to go in."

Slowly, they approached the school. It looked as dark and empty as it did on any weekend. Stopping in front, the lumpy king tried the doors. They swung open.

"So," he said, "someone *is* in here. In the interest of our safety, I'll enter first."

"And in the interest of *my* safety," murmured Neal, "I'll enter last. . . ."

One by one, the friends filed into the school, first Khan, then Julie, then Keeah and Max.

Just as Eric put his hand on the door, he felt something wet and warm strike his neck. Looking up, he saw someone pull back from the edge of the roof and out of sight.

"Hey, who is that?" he shouted. "Who's up there? Show yourself!"

There was no answer.

"That's twice, you know," whispered Neal, scanning the empty roof. "Someone really is spying on us. It makes me think of the new girl."

The new girl.

For the past few weeks, Eric, Julie, and Neal had suspected that a new girl in their neighborhood had been spying on them. Her name was Meredith. She seemed to be around whenever they talked about Droon.

She might have already heard them.

Eric squinted up at the roof. "If she was up there, she's gone now. We have to remember our mission: Find Sparr."

"Right. Find Sparr," repeated Neal. "And get him back to Droon before he gives Gethwing what he wants. Come on."

Taking a deep breath, Eric pulled open the school doors, and the two friends went in together.

Outside, the sun had been bright and hot, but the hallways inside were dark, cool, and quiet.

Khan was already far down the hall, sniffing constantly. "My nose tells me . . . we turn to the left. Sparr could be near. I'm not sure, so be careful, now."

The troop pushed farther into the darkness, their footsteps echoing against the walls.

"Do you think Sparr really doesn't know what Gethwing is looking for?" asked Julie.

"Ever since he became young, he's been remembering more and more of what he knew as a boy."

"Maybe," said Eric. "I don't remember all that much from when I was really young, but then, not everyone is a son of Zara like Sparr is. Maybe that helps him to remember."

"I don't remember much, either," added Neal. "Except for the picnics and barbecues, of course. Which reminds me of my first chili dog —"

"Neal, hush!" hissed Khan suddenly. "Hide!"

They all dived behind an open door and peered into a large room nearby. There were dozens of tables set out across the floor and a long counter running along the back wall.

"The cafeteria," whispered Julie.

Neal sighed. "Did I ever tell you about the first time I had lunch here —"

"Look at that!" interrupted Keeah.

A single dark figure was moving along the counter in the back, then stopped. There came the soft creak of a metal cabinet followed by a quiet rattle of plates.

A moment later, the figure, cloaked all in black, stood up. It held something white in its hands and said, "I've found it!"

"Oh, my gosh!" whispered Eric. "It's Sparr! And he's found the magic thing!"

The friends ran into the room at once.

"Sparr!" cried Keeah. "If you've found what Gethwing is after —"

The boy jumped back, surprised. "What? No!" He put the white thing into his mouth and began to chew.

Neal gaped. "Wait a minute. You're eating? What is that? Angel food cake?"

"I was hungry!" said Sparr. "I haven't eaten since I left Droon two days ago —"

"Two days!" gasped Eric. "You mean . . . it's Monday?"

"A school day?" said Neal. "And there's no school? Wow, time really *has* passed."

"And a lot has happened," said Sparr, shoving the rest of the cake into his mouth. "Look what I found." He darted across the room to a portable table and rolled it aside.

Where the wall would normally be was a ragged opening to a narrow passage.

Beyond the passage the kids saw a landscape of scorched and rocky earth that stretched for miles and miles. It was pelted by rain that fell from a sky crackling with lightning and booming with thunder.

"What is that?" gasped Julie. "*Where* is that?"

Not far beyond the passage, a band of

knights in armor stood side by side. They were tall, thin, and bearded, and they seemed very old. Their armor, including helmets and shields, was worn and rusty.

Max's large troll eyes grew even larger. "Are they who we heard marching?"

"Probably," said Sparr.

"Are they . . . ghosts?" asked Neal.

Sparr laughed softly. "Not yet. They're all that remain of the Ancient Knights of Pim."

"They're ancient, all right," said Julie. "They can barely stand!"

Sparr nodded. "Long ago, they were a fierce and evil army in your — our — world. They numbered in the millions. My mother, Zara, heard about the knights. There were too many to defeat, but she charmed them to obey only her. She ordered them to leave our world and live happily. I think they did, until now. How

Gethwing discovered them, I can't say. But he must have learned my mother's charm. He commanded the remaining knights to help him. Even though they don't want to, they have to."

The knights wobbled on their feet as they tried to stand at attention.

Keeah shook her head in disbelief. "It looks like they've aged a lot since then. Where are they? *Under* the school?"

"Not under the school," said Neal, sitting up suddenly. "Next to the school. I know that place. It's the shadow world. It's Calibaz!"

"Score one for Neal," said Sparr. "It is Calibaz. Or what *used* to be Calibaz."

Calibaz was the mysterious city that the kids had once discovered next to their world. It was separated from the real world and kept invisible by a strange and magical veil. Calibaz was a gray, unhappy place. It was like a gloomy shadow of the real world. The hills, valleys, trees, even the ocean in Calibaz were like those in the rest of the Upper World, but without the light, the towns, or the people.

As Eric gazed into the passage, he remembered that Calibaz was where he had first seen the Moon Medallion. Little did he know then just how important it would turn out to be.

All of a sudden, there came the rumbling and squeaking of giant wheels. A moment later a long train of wagons rolled into view, and men, women, children, friends, parents, teachers — everyone from the town — was crammed inside.

"My gosh!" murmured Julie. "I see my parents! Neal, your parents! They're — prisoners!"

The squeaky wagons were being rolled

across the black ground and into the distance by a second troop of knights.

Before too long — *fwap-fwap-fwap!* — Gethwing swooped down from the rainy sky and landed in the midst of the knights. Tossing a large, heavy bag to the ground, he growled, "Two more to add to the rest!"

The bag wriggled and twisted and finally tore open, and two figures jumped out. One held a club and wore a flannel shirt. The other had long blond hair.

Keeah gasped. "Mother! Father!"

"You won't get away with this!" yelled Zello as the knights chained him and Relna to the others in the last wagon.

"The children will fight you!" said Relna.

Gethwing laughed menacingly. "Silence, prisoners! Knights, take them to Blackdark Castle and put them in the dungeon with everyone else. *Now!*"

Three

The Shadow Land

"To Blackdark Castle!" repeated a wiry old knight with a long gray beard. He pointed a wobbly hand into the distance.

"Blackdark Castle?" said Neal as the last wagon rolled noisily away. "Is that lame, or what?"

"Maybe it's lame," said Sparr, "but for the last two days they've been rounding up people and taking them there. And now they've got almost everyone."

"Except us," said Julie. "And, if you don't mind, I'd like to keep it that way."

"Moon dragon," the old knight said. "You summoned us from the mountains to help you. The town is now empty. We are old and tired. Let us go home."

"Trust me, I will let you leave," said Gethwing, holding his claw over the knights as if he were controlling them. "As soon as I have what I came to find. Do one more thing, then you may go."

"Tell us, and we must obey," said the old knight, bowing. When he tried to rise, he couldn't straighten out his back, so several other knights helped him up.

Gethwing glared at the little troop, muttering under his breath. "The legend says, 'A boy will find it.' I have opened this veil so that you may return to the town. Go find the boy, and bring him to me!"

The knight grumbled, "Knights of Pim, we must obey! To town once more!"

The troop of old armored men turned to the passage and moved toward it in a slow march. *Stomp . . . stomp . . .*

Gethwing growled, "March faster!"

The tall knight turned. "This *is* fast for us. We're a thousand years old, you know!"

"We'd better hide," said Eric. "The knights' eyesight may not be good, but we can't risk them seeing us."

Together the children, Max, and Khan ducked behind a long cafeteria table.

The knights moved slowly past the tables, out the doors, and through the halls to the front of the school.

A moment later, the veil blurred and the passage to Calibaz vanished, leaving a normal kitchen wall in its place.

Max gulped. "Now what?"

"Well," said Neal, "I don't know how

many veils there are, but I know at least one other one. *And* I know how to open it."

Julie smiled. "Of course! Pikoo's horn!"

Pikoo's horn. On the kids' last visit to Calibaz, they had met a mysterious and friendly tribe of froglike creatures called hoobahs. Among them was the kids' special friend Pikoo. When the right tune was played on Pikoo's strange horn, the veil between the worlds lifted away, allowing the kids to enter and leave Calibaz whenever they wanted. Pikoo had left his horn in the real world, and Neal had it.

"I say we use the horn to find our families and free them," said Neal, "and then send those retired knights back to Pim. Wherever that is."

"Good plan," said Sparr.

Khan beamed. "That gets my vote!"

"And mine," chirped Max.

Keeah smiled. "Sounds like it's time for a little veil music!"

"Follow me!" said Neal.

In moments the little group worked its way out of the school and into the streets, careful to stay clear of the old knights.

A few minutes later, they arrived at Neal's house. Since it was empty, Neal rushed upstairs and was down in a second with the strange little horn. It was large at one end and small at the other, with tiny finger holes down the length of it.

"Do you remember the tune, Neal?" asked Eric.

Neal looked at the horn and smiled. "Not a day goes by when I don't hear it playing in my head. I've wanted to go back to Calibaz a thousand times. Now there's a reason. Come on."

The friends ran quickly to the center of town, where they entered a narrow alley between the pizza place and the dry cleaners. At the end of the alley stood a solid brick wall.

"The knights are coming," said Khan, sniffing over his shoulder. "I sense them shuffling down the street. We need to hurry."

Closing his eyes, Neal put the little horn to his mouth and blew softly into it. *Weee-ooo-e-o-e-o-e-ooo!* The tune sounded half like a breeze blowing through the leaves and half like the gurgle of water in a stream.

"So strange," said Sparr.

"And beautiful!" said Max.

All at once, the air quivered in front of them. It reminded Eric of waves moving slowly across the surface of the pond. "I still can't believe a whole shadow world exists right next to ours," he said.

"Here it comes," whispered Julie.

A moment later, the rough wall that closed off the alley wasn't there. In its place, the kids saw a strange but familiar world of dark hills and trees, jagged rocks, and steady, pelting rain.

"Calibaz!" said Khan.

Without another word, the little band pushed their way through the quivering air and into the shadow world.

As bright as the day had been in town, the sky over Calibaz was nearly black.

"It reminds me of the Dark Lands," said Sparr under his breath. "What a place . . ."

"And our parents are in here some-where," said Keeah. "Prisoners."

Eric looked at her. "We'll find them. All of them."

"Excuse me, I'm getting a bit soggy here," said Khan, squinting up into the rain. "Let's keep moving."

"He's right," said Sparr, tightening his cloak as he turned. "One thing I know how to find is a castle with a dungeon. I practically invented them." Then, leaping over the puddles and streams that crisscrossed the rutted ground, he moved off stealthily into the darkness.

The rest of the group followed Sparr, until, a little while later, he stopped.

"Well, that was easy," said Sparr, pointing straight ahead. "Blackdark Castle. It has Gethwing written all over it."

Barely visible in the darkness stood the shadow of a castle with a giant dragon's head peering down from its highest tower.

Neal grumbled, "Blackdark Castle may be a lame name, but I guess Gethwing got it right. Here come our parents."

A line of wagons was being wheeled through a gate and into the castle.

"And here *he* comes," said Keeah at the

sound of flapping wings echoing through the air.

The kids ducked behind a craggy rock as Gethwing swooped down toward the gate. When the wagon disappeared inside the castle, the dragon followed it in, and the gate shut with a tremendous *boom*.

"Guess where we're going," said Max.

"Guess who's not first," added Neal.

"Come on, everyone," said Sparr.

The friends paused for a second, then rushed together through the rain toward the very black, very dark Blackdark Castle.

Four

A Little Fireside Chat

The closer the kids, Max, and Khan got to Blackdark Castle, the more it loomed up before them, a terrifying shadow against the dark sky.

"Look," said Julie, pointing up at a thin coil of dark air near the castle's dragon head. "Smoke."

"Julie, I like the way you think," said Neal. "You think that where there's smoke, there's food, and where there's food —"

"No, Neal," said Julie. "I think that where there's smoke, there's a chimney, and where there's a chimney, there's a way in. We can't just walk in the front door, you know."

Neal shrugged. "I knew that."

Eric glanced up the side of the castle. The walls were jagged in places, and extremely dangerous-looking. "I don't know. . . ."

"Don't worry," said Julie. "I can fly us to the top. Once we're there, we can climb down inside the shaft."

"Good idea," said Sparr. "But I hope the fire is low. I may shoot sparks, but I really don't want to land in any!"

Everyone held hands, and Julie flew them carefully up the side of the castle.

Once at the top, the children paused for a moment to catch their breath. Far below, the black sea was churning with whitecaps. In the opposite direction, where they knew their town was in reality, were ranges of bare black hills.

To Eric, the view was frightening and sad. "This is what our world would look like if you took away the things that make it our world."

"Everybody, look. The other veils," said Julie, pointing to five shimmering veils at different points in the distance. "Our two worlds really do connect. A lot."

"Three worlds," said Sparr. "Remember the pit?" He looked down at where the ground was dug away in an open and raw pit. "At the bottom of that is a hole that leads from Calibaz right down to the Dark Lands of Droon."

Eric remembered the pit. Back when Sparr was evil, he had forced the poor hoobahs of Calibaz to dig a hole through the earth that opened right over his terrible volcano palace.

"Okay, that's enough sightseeing, everyone," said Keeah. "Into the castle. To the dungeon. We have people to rescue!"

The seven friends scurried together across the dragon-headed castle roof. In the center was the large round opening of a chimney. Only a very thin wisp of smoke drifted up from it now.

"Good thing it's not lunchtime," said Max.

"What?" said Neal, alarmed. "Oh, right. I see what you mean."

Peering down, they saw openings all the way down the shaft, where the castle's many hearths joined the main chimney. From the very bottom came the dull glow of embers and the echo of voices.

In no time, Max spun several ropes from spider silk. Using them, the friends began the careful climb down the chimney. They were ten feet down, then twenty

feet, when a raspy voice echoed up the shaft.

"Light! Gethwing needs more light!"

Then the children heard the tread of slow footsteps and what sounded like wood being dragged across a floor. Finally, they saw logs heaved into the hearth and sparks and flakes of black ash flying.

"Guys!" hissed Keeah. "I think we need to get out of this chimney — right now!"

An instant later — *whoomf!* — flames began roaring straight up the shaft.

"We'll be fried!" cried Eric.

"Toasted, actually!" said Max. "Back up!"

"Into a side passage," said Sparr. "Here!"

The kids scrambled after Sparr into the nearest opening they could find.

"Akkk!" squeaked Neal. "Could we have picked a smaller place to hide? Whose foot is in my back?"

"It's not one of mine!" cried Max.

"It's your own!" snapped Julie.

"No wonder it hurts!" said Neal.

"Shhh!" hissed Eric. "Those knights may be old, but they still have ears!"

"Hey, look what I found," said Sparr.

Neal squirmed to look. "More cake?"

"Better!" said Sparr. "Right . . . here . . ."

There was a *squeak* and a *thud*, and suddenly, Sparr slid out of the chimney and into the fireplace of a small room. Everyone tumbled after him just as the shaft filled with black smoke.

"Nice work, Sparr," said Julie.

The boy grinned. "Only the best for my friends. And look, a room with a view!"

When they stood up, the friends found themselves in a small, empty room with an opening that looked over the hall below.

"We can find out what Gethwing is up to!" said Keeah. "Let's listen."

Crouching by the opening, they peered

down into a giant black room lit with wall torches. Directly below them stood the great fireplace, now blazing with flames.

Hanging on the wall opposite were two swords, one crossed over the other.

"Those swords," said Sparr. "They look so familiar. . . ."

"*They* look familiar, too," said Khan, pointing. "Here come the knights. Slowly, as usual."

A long line of ancient knights filed into the room. A minute, two minutes, ten minutes later, they stopped. One knight stepped forward, tried to bow, then gave up.

"All hail Gethwing!" he said sullenly.

Moments later, the moon dragon strode into the room. He looked angry, thrashing his tail across the floor as he paced.

"You have taken all the people," he said. "All the houses are empty, everything is there for the taking, and still you didn't find the boy. There's no sign of what I seek! My time is running out. I need the Pearl Sea!"

Sparr gasped. "The Pearl Sea . . ."

The children turned to him.

"Is that what Gethwing wants you to find?" asked Keeah. "What is it?"

The boy stood very still, not breathing. "I see . . . I see . . ." Finally, he shook his head. "I don't know. All I see is . . . little bits of black ash flying around, like in the chimney. Sorry."

"I must have the Pearl!" snarled the moon dragon below. "If it's in the town, *someone* must know. Bring me the prisoners. I'll question them one by one if I have to. Quickly!"

The old knight blinked. "Quickly? We can't do anything quickly, you know."

Gethwing roared, "Enough! I should have done this from the beginning." He narrowed his eyes and glanced around at the knights. "When you were young, you were a great fighting force. And there were so many of you. So . . . how would you like to be young again?"

The dragon spun around and grabbed one of the swords crossed on the wall.

"Those swords," whispered Sparr. "He's going to reverse my mother's charm!"

Gethwing raised the sword high over the knights and began to utter strange, low words. At once, the blade flashed with light, the hearth fire blazed, and the knights' armor began to change color.

Eric felt almost dizzy watching it.

From rusty red, the armor turned muddy brown, then gray, and finally black. At the same time, the knights grew larger, their faces became hard and dark, and their eyes turned bright red.

"This is *so* not good," said Sparr.

"You are now the Blackdark Knights of

Blackdark Castle!" boomed Gethwing. "You are finally fit to be my army. Go, call your fellow knights from every part of the shadow land. We shall need a huge army for what I have planned!"

The chief knight stepped forward. He slapped his breastplate loudly. "Knights!" he shouted in a deep voice. "We shall conquer this world! Now — bring in the prisoners as Gethwing commands. Go! Double time!"

As the knights trotted from the room, Eric knew as he never had before that Gethwing possessed the power to turn good to evil. Would he — *could* he — do the same to Sparr?

Moments later, the chief knight was back. "Your majesty! The first prisoner!"

Pinned in an iron grasp between two large knights was a woman with brown hair, wriggling to free herself. The knights pushed her in front of the moon dragon.

Gethwing held his claw out to her.

"Raise your head," he said.

The woman trembled as she lifted her face to the dragon.

Eric nearly choked in shock. "Mom!"

Five

The Wizard's Mom

The knights stood at attention around Mrs. Hinkle. Gethwing strode back and forth, glaring down at her with his smoldering red eyes. "So . . . I know things about people. You are the mother of that boy Eric. Do you know about him? Do you know who your son is?"

Eric's heart leaped into his throat. He watched his mother look up at the dragon, quivering under his gaze, but saying nothing.

Gethwing raised himself to his full height. "Have you ever heard . . . of the Pearl Sea?"

"The Pearl . . . the Pearl Sea . . ." she said, as if in a trance. "I *have* heard of it. . . ."

Eric stared at his mother, his heart throbbing faster and faster. "Mom?" he whispered under his breath, "My gosh. Whatever you know, don't tell him!"

"Yesssss!" hissed Gethwing, lowering his giant head down to her. His evil grin reached from ear to ear. "Tell me where it is —"

She met the dragon's fiery gaze and said firmly, "It's the Japanese restaurant behind the library, isn't it?"

"Yes!" whispered Neal. "You tell him, Mrs. H!"

Gethwing roared with rage. "No! You are his mother! Don't tell me you don't know! Your son, Eric Hinkle, is . . . a wizard!"

"Uh-oh," Eric murmured.

Mrs. Hinkle stepped back suddenly. Her mouth hung open. She quivered from head to foot. Once more she raised her eyes to meet Gethwing's.

"Eric . . . is a . . . wizard?" she asked.

"He is!" said the dragon.

She trembled for a moment, then breathed deeply. "So why can't he clean his room?"

"Oh, snap!" whispered Julie. "She is awesome!"

When Gethwing roared, raising the sword over Mrs. Hinkle, Eric felt his blood boil. "You hurt her, you big scaly creep, and I swear, I'll —"

"I'll do it," said Sparr softly. He turned toward the chimney. "I'll go down there."

"What? You can't go down there," said Keeah. "Gethwing is looking for *you*. Let's just blast him from here —"

But the boy was already crawling back into the chimney. "No, look. I have a better idea. I'm the one he wants. He thinks I know where this Pearl Sea is? Well, I'll trick him. I'll take him on a wild ride. You guys free the people and get them ready for a battle like you've never seen. And Eric, don't leave without those swords. There's something about them —"

"Sparr!" chirped Max. "You can't go!"

"I have to," said Sparr. "But I'll send you a signal when Gethwing's coming —"

"What kind of signal?" asked Neal.

"A *signal*!" snapped Sparr. "Now go. Save your parents. Go!" He vanished into the shaft.

As the kids, Max, and Khan watched from above, Gethwing moved closer and closer to Mrs. Hinkle with the sword. Just then, Sparr made a sudden, loud noise in the chimney.

"Owww!" he cried. "That's hot!"

He crashed down onto the burning logs in an explosion of sparks and smoke, then tumbled out of the chimney and into the room, rolling across the floor to Gethwing's feet.

"Sparr!" the moon dragon gasped.

The boy coughed and blinked and waved away the smoke. "Uh-oh. Wrong room! Just pretend I'm not here. Excuse me —"

"Seize him!" Gethwing shrieked.

Before the boy could move, thirty dark knights closed in around him. The moon dragon advanced on Sparr, his eyes blazing like fire.

Sparr struggled against the knights for a

moment, then stopped. Trying to sound as if he had no choice but to tell, he said, "All right, all right. I know where the Pearl Sea is." He motioned to Mrs. Hinkle. "That lady doesn't know anything. Let her go back to the others. Forget the sword, too. Its power is nothing compared to the Pearl Sea. I'll show you. But you'd better wear your boots. The Pearl Sea is down by the coast. I hid it under the water behind a big rock."

Gethwing stared at Sparr, then howled with laughter. He slid the sword back onto the wall and flicked his claw at Eric's mother. "Take this prisoner back to the others," he boomed. "She's of no use to me."

As two knights took away Mrs. Hinkle, Gethwing stormed from the room, saying, "Bring the boy. We go to the coast!"

Eric couldn't take his eyes off Sparr as the remaining knights pulled him roughly after the dragon.

"I can't believe it," said Julie. "Sparr was incredible. He let Gethwing catch him in order to save our parents!"

"Incredible," said Eric, still staring down.

Keeah pulled his arm lightly. "There's going to be a battle before this is all over. We need our parents. Come on."

Finally tearing himself away, Eric scrambled out of the room and followed his friends.

Six

Dungeon of Dungeons

After Gethwing and the knights marched Sparr away, the kids, Max, and Khan snuck down into the great empty room.

Eric pulled the two swords from the wall. After slicing them both around in the air, he tucked one in his belt. "For Sparr, when we see him again. And we *will* see him."

Keeah nodded. "We've gone too far to

let Gethwing have him for good. But first, our parents. Let's go."

"This way," said Khan, moving quickly into the passages. The wall torches grew fewer and fewer as the friends went deeper into the castle. Shadows and darkness surrounded them more with every step.

"Again, I'm thinking Gethwing chose the perfect name for his creepy little place," said Neal. "Blackdark? Oh, yeah."

The group moved through the passages until they came to a long tunnel that ended at a tall black door. Four giant knights were standing guard in front of it. Each one was holding a seven-foot-long spear.

The friends all looked at one another.

"Together?" said Khan.

"Together," everyone replied at once.

The six friends crept down the tunnel as carefully as possible. When they were a few feet from the black door, they all whispered for a second, nodded, and jumped out of hiding.

"Ayeeee!" they screamed.

The knights lunged forward instantly, but Eric and Keeah had already flattened themselves to the floor. They blasted silver and violet sparks at the knights' feet.

"Owww!" the four knights cried. When they tumbled to the floor, Neal, Khan, and Julie jumped on top of their backs while Max sprayed a thick, sticky web of spider silk over them. The struggle was over in a moment. The knights were wrapped like mummies.

Wasting no time, Eric and Keeah blasted the black door off its hinges and charged through. They stopped instantly. Before them was a room that seemed to go on forever. In it stood thousands of townspeople, crowded together in the dark.

"Uh, excuse me," said Keeah, "but I think we're here to save you?"

At once, the crowd erupted in cheers whose echoes filled the passages of the castle.

Eric rushed to his parents. Julie's and Neal's came running to them. The king and queen hugged Keeah tightly.

"We have no time to waste," said Max. "Everyone out. Two at a time, please!"

"What happened to the old knights?" asked Julie's mother as they pushed into the outer passage. "They seemed nice."

"They changed," said Julie. "And not just their armor. Gethwing cursed them."

"This way!" said Khan as he and Max led everyone into the passage. "That's right, ma'am. I'm a talking pillow —"

"Khan, can you sniff our way back through the castle and out again?" asked Keeah.

The lumpy king nodded firmly. "I can. People, look sharp and follow me. Max?"

"Here, as always!" said the spider troll.

The townspeople followed Khan and Max through the passages. Halfway back in the crowd were Julie and Neal, while Eric and Keeah stayed at the dungeon to make sure no one was left behind.

Once the last person exited the dungeon, the two friends followed. But when they came to a place where the passage split, Eric stopped. The crowd hustled down one tunnel. But he saw wet footprints across the floor of the other.

"Keeah, wait," he said. "It's that girl, Meredith. She's been spying on us all day. I'm sure of it. And now she's here —"

"Yes, I'm here," said a voice. Suddenly, Meredith moved out of the shadows. She was soaking wet, as if she had just come in from the rain.

Eric gasped. "I knew it. It was you at the pond, wasn't it?"

"And on the school roof," she said.

"But how did you get on this side of the veil?" he asked. "Where did you come from? I've never seen your parents, even though you live right down the street from me. Who even *are* you?"

Meredith fixed her dark eyes on him. "Eric, if this is a quiz, maybe I could take it later. There's no time now. More knights are coming. Lots of them. Sparr was right — the real battle hasn't begun yet."

"Sparr?" said Keeah. "You know about him?"

The girl turned away. "Just come on. I need to show you something." She darted down the second tunnel and was gone.

Eric stared after her, then turned to Keeah. "This is really weird, you know."

"No kidding," said the princess, listening

for sounds behind them. "But maybe she's right. We should get out of here."

"Excuse me? Tick-tock?" Meredith's voice came from down the tunnel.

"Coming!" called Eric.

Together, the two wizards raced from one passage to another, just behind Meredith, until they were finally outside. The great crowd of townspeople, with Khan and Max in the lead, was safely heading toward the main veil.

Eric couldn't stop staring at the dark-haired girl. He cleared his throat. "At the pond before, you were underwater for a long time. How did you do that? How is that even possible?"

"Never mind what's possible and what's not," Meredith said, looking around before moving on. "I can't explain everything yet, so don't ask me. What I do know is that when Gethwing turned those old knights into his Blackdark Knights, he somehow woke all their friends from across the shadow land. Look —"

In the far-off mountains were dark masses of knights moving slowly toward them.

"Knights are coming," said Meredith. "A million of them. Maybe more."

Eric began shaking his head. "Oh, no."

"Oh, yes," said the girl. "Gethwing called them to this one spot. There are five veils here. Your town is the only place where beings from the shadow world can enter your world."

"Your world, too," said Keeah.

"Sure, my world, too," said the girl.

Eric's heart thudded in his chest. "So how can we stop them?"

Meredith didn't answer. She stooped to a narrow stream that wound across the path. "This stream leads to one of the veils.

Eric, wait here. I need to check some-thing. Kee . . ."

"Keeah," said the princess.

"Right," said the girl. "Come with me. Eric, you stay here. Try to figure out how long we have before the knights arrive."

Keeah looked at Eric, made a face, then followed the girl away among the rocks.

Eric stood next to a cluster of trees and stared at the distant mountains. The mas-sive army of dark knights was marching closer with each passing minute.

Eric's heart sank. "There *are* millions of them. There *will* be a battle —"

Just then, his eye happened to glance at the tree he was standing next to. He knew that Calibaz was a mere shadow of his own world, but he recognized the tree as a duplicate of one that stood right outside his house.

Laying his hand on the lowermost

branch, Eric was overcome with a sudden surge of energy. He staggered but did not let go of the tree. His knees felt weak, and his mind was seized with a powerful image.

Closing his eyes, he saw himself as a very small boy, sitting on that same tree branch. He was looking back at his house, humming idly to himself, when he had a sudden sense of a figure moving behind him. Turning slowly, he made out the shape of someone standing in a gleam of light. Then he felt something small drop into his open hand. He held up his palm and looked into it. "Wow!" he said in his young voice. "Thanks!"

"Eric," said Keeah, suddenly close by. "Are you all right?"

"Huh?" He popped open his eyes and let go of the tree. Keeah was standing next to him.

He looked in his palm.

It was empty.

"The strange girl is gone," said the princess. "One minute she's here, the next she's not. It's very weird. But she did show me a way out. Everyone is through the veil and heading for the school. The girl said again that there would be a battle. We need to be there —"

Eric looked into Keeah's face, and he began shaking his head. "No. No, Keeah, we need to go to my house. It's where the Pearl Sea is. Don't ask me how I know — I just do. We need to go there. Now!"

Seven

The Pearl Sea

The veil was nearly closed when —
whoosh! — the two friends ran through,
only to find thousands of people gathering
with the king, queen, Neal, Julie, Khan, and
Max at the school.

"Let's drive our cars around the school!"
shouted Julie's father. "We'll form a wall!"

"Rakes!" yelled Neal's mother. "We can
fight them with rakes. Brooms, too!"

"Our army," whispered Eric, seeing his

mother and father among the crowd. He wanted to go to them, to make sure they were okay. But his mind still reeled with a vision he didn't understand.

"They're all getting ready," said Keeah.

"And we'll help," said Eric. "But first I need you to come with me. Hurry, before my mom sees me and asks me about the wizard thing."

"I'm right with you!" Keeah said, running down Main Street next to him. "Do you know yet what the Pearl Sea is?"

Gripping both swords firmly as he ran, Eric shook his head. "Every minute I think I remember more, the vision begins to fade. Sorry, I just don't know."

Eric passed into his yard, looking along the left side of the house. Yes, the tallest tree was the same one he saw in Calibaz. Inside, his house was eerily empty. Wandering through the kitchen, living room, dining room, even bathroom, he found himself again and again at the base of the steps leading to the second floor.

"Eric?" said Keeah, searching his face.

He raised his eyes to the top step. "It's up there," he said. Sliding both swords into his belt and taking a deep breath, he climbed the stairs steadily. Turning right, he stood in the doorway of his bedroom. Dresser, bed, desk. His clothes were strewn across the rug.

"Your mom was right," said Keeah.

"I know it's a mess," he said. "But what we're looking for isn't in here."

Over the sound of his own heart beating, he heard the townspeople outside preparing for the coming battle. Soon the dark army would be there. Soon the terrible fight would begin.

"Keeah, this is nuts," he said, turning back to the stairs. "They need us —"

"No!" she said. "Eric, this is important. If the Pearl Sea is here, you need to find it."

He shut his eyes again but opened them just as quickly. "I can't concentrate."

Keeah looked at him. "Maybe you need . . . I mean . . . I could put you into a trance —"

"Yes!" said Eric. "Yes, do it! Just don't make me do anything dumb. I don't want to jump around like a monkey or anything."

Keeah smiled. "Oh, no. I'm saving that spell for another time."

"What?"

"Eric, just close your eyes. This won't hurt."

"I hope not," he said with a laugh. When he closed his eyes, Keeah began to murmur under her breath. *"Mai-no . . . pareethlah . . . chaylee-sol . . ."*

At once, the sounds from outside began

to drift away from Eric. The clattering of sticks, the yelling, the sound of cars surrounding the school — all grew quiet.

And there in the darkness behind his eyelids shone a pale silvery light. Was it the sun in his eyes? No. It was moonlight.

Again, the moon, he thought. *What's with the moon? Moon Medallion. Moon dragon. Always the moon!*

And there he was, small again, sitting in that same tree by the side of his house. It was . . . what? Eight years ago? Nine? He was very small. He sat perfectly still on the branch, humming softly to himself when, all of a sudden, something moved near him. Some*one* moved. Above Keeah's whispering came the person's quiet words.

Eric . . . here . . .

The voice . . . it made him feel . . . what was it? The voice made him feel . . . *safe.*

Then he felt something drop into his hand.

He saw it lying there.

And he knew.

Suddenly, his eyes popped open. He left the trance completely.

"What is it?" asked Keeah.

Without answering, Eric walked down the hall to his parents' room. He opened his mother's closet and set his foot on the lowest shelf to boost himself to the top. There, he found a small wooden chest. He couldn't remember ever seeing it before, but he knew exactly what it was. He grabbed it and jumped back to the floor.

"Keeah," he said, "I'm afraid."

"I guess that makes two of us," she said. "But it's okay. We're in this together, Eric."

"Yeah," he said softly. "Thanks."

He opened the chest slowly. Inside it

was a small blue velvet box. Tilting the tiny box open, Eric saw a white gem the size of a marble.

"Oh my gosh!" whispered Keeah. "That's it. It actually *is* a pearl. It's beautiful!"

The Pearl really is *beautiful*, thought Eric. It was milky white, with swirls of brighter white across its surface. No, not across its surface. The closer he looked, the more Eric realized that the swirls were coming from *inside* the Pearl. Staring closer still, he saw that the swirls were moving around inside the gem, like whitecapped waves rising and crashing in a great ocean.

"The Pearl Sea!" he murmured softly.

Keeah looked at him. "Eric, the old legend was about you. *You* were the boy to find it. Not Sparr."

Eric thought about the prophecy that Gethwing was following. "I guess that's true. But I don't have a clue about what the Pearl

Sea is. I think I got it when I was little. Really little. But I don't know what it means. My mom might —"

There was the sudden sound of marching feet outside the window. The waves on the Pearl dissolved, and the inside of the tiny orb was filled with swirling black flakes, falling and falling.

"Black snow!" murmured Eric. "That's what Sparr talked about —"

At that moment, a boy's wild shout echoed through the streets. "Signal! Signal! Hey, everybody — this is the *SIGNAL!*"

Eric and Keeah looked at each other.

"Sparr's back —" said Eric.

Keeah nodded. "And Gethwing can't be far behind!"

"Let's go!"

Eight

Face-off at the School

Sliding the Pearl securely into his pocket, Eric drew his sword, and ran with Keeah straight for the school. The moment they got there, the two friends came to a dead stop.

"Holy cow!" gasped Eric.

"You can say that again," added Keeah.

"Holy cow!" Eric repeated.

The mass of people they had seen before had changed. Now the parking lot in front of the school was filled with townspeople standing side by side at attention. Each man, woman, and child among them was armed like a warrior. They held bats, hockey sticks, tree branches, rakes, brooms, and mops. They wore bike helmets, football helmets, and hockey masks. They carried trash-can lids like shields.

King Zello, Queen Relna, Julie, Neal, Khan, and Max were facing the crowd from the school's front steps.

"Eric," said Keeah. "This is amazing. These are your parents, neighbors, teachers, friends. They really *are* an army."

"They . . . they . . . love our town," Eric said, barely getting the words out.

As they wormed their way to the front of the crowd, the two kids passed Mrs. Tracy and Mr. Frando, Eric's teachers. They passed Mrs. Kroger, Neal's mother, the town librarian. Finally, they found Eric's parents in the front line of defenders.

"Mom, Dad, you're safe!" he said.

They hugged him tightly.

"Eric, that dragon called you a wizard," said Mrs. Hinkle.

Eric gulped. "Oh, Mom," he said. "You know you can't trust dragons!"

His father gave him a smile, "I don't know what's going on, son," he said. "Maybe you do. But we'll fight to protect our little family and save our town."

Eric smiled back. "Thanks, Dad."

He turned to his mother. His hand went to the Pearl in his pocket. "Mom —"

Just then, Sparr broke through the crowd. Eric and the others rushed to him.

"You're okay!" said Keeah.

"Barely," said Sparr, out of breath. "I stayed inches ahead of Gethwing. And

I mean *inches*. Look!" He swung his cloak around. There were claw marks down the back of it. "I held him off for as long as I could. But there he is! And he's mad!" He pointed up. The moon dragon was circling very high over the school.

"He figured out that I was tricking him," Sparr added. "I'm sorry —"

"No," said Relna. "You gave us time to escape and to arm for battle."

"And you gave me time to find it," added Eric quietly.

Sparr turned. "You found the Pearl Sea?"

For an instant, Eric imagined that he saw Sparr's fins turn from purple to black. He opened his palm. The Pearl sat in the middle of it.

Sparr stared openmouthed at the gem, but the swirling shapes Eric had seen before were frozen and unmoving on its surface.

Before they could say more, there came

the sudden sound of feet thundering in step from inside the school.

"Steady!" boomed Zello. "Here come the knights!"

Eric gave Sparr the sword from his belt, raised his own, and joined the others in the front line.

"Son, you be careful with that sword," said Mr. Hinkle. "It looks very dangerous."

"The moon dragon is dangerous, Dad," Eric replied. "But yeah, I'll be careful —"

Thump! Thump!

Everyone backed away as the first black-armored knights burst out the doors and assembled on the front steps. The knights seemed more fearsome than ever.

"Be ready," whispered Keeah, looking right and left. "We can do this."

"Together," said Queen Relna, standing next to the king.

Khan unwound the gold cord that

decorated his shoulders. Holding it in his hands, he leaned toward the spider troll. "What do you say, Max? A little contest to see who can stop more knights?"

Max looked grim as he spun a stout rope with a loop on one end. "The loser treats both to a full Jaffa City breakfast?"

"With gizzleberry muffins?"

"It's not breakfast without gizzleberries," chirped Max. "You're on, Khan!"

There was a terrible moment of silence, when the knights and the townspeople stared at each other. An instant later, the parking lot was a battlefield.

Clang! Boomf! Clonk!

Zello bolted forward first, single-handedly flinging a troop of knights into the bike racks. Relna led a wave of broom-wielding townspeople after a squad of knights pushing toward the playground.

Keeah blasted with her sparking fingers,

then charged. Eric's blade flashed brightly as he swung it, sending knights retreating through the school doors. "Save our town!" he cried.

Sparr waded through the attackers, his own sword blazing against their shields. *Clank! Bong!*

Julie and Neal battled forward together with their parents, forcing more knights back into the school.

"Yes, push them inside!" cried Relna, as she and Zello charged with the rest of the townspeople. They were soon through the doors.

"Ha-ha!" cried Max as two knights got their feet tangled in his rope and fell outside the main office. "Four and five!"

"Sorry, Max, but you're already behind!" said Khan as he whipped his golden cord around the knees of a trio of growling knights. "This makes eight for me!"

From one hallway to the next, from one classroom to the other, the brave townspeople swatted with mops and battered with brooms. The entire high school softball team clobbered the knights' shields with aluminum bats, sending them deeper into the school.

"Fourteen!" Max yelped, tangling three large knights in a sticky web.

"We're tied!" cheered Khan, whipping his tasseled cord back into his hand. "Keep going!"

The battle raged into the gym, where a troop of knights had cornered some parents. Neal and Julie charged in to help, only to find the parents swinging tennis rackets and lacrosse sticks and pummeling the knights with volleyballs and tennis balls.

"Score!" yelled Mrs. Kroger, as the knights fled into the halls.

Neal grinned. "Let's win this game!"

Grabbing the equipment, he and Julie helped their parents push the knights all the way up two sets of stairs to the roof.

As the battle poured across the rooftop, Julie flew overhead, pelting the armored troops with volleyballs, while Neal slammed tennis balls at them. Keeah joined in, blasting at the knights with Relna and Zello by her side.

All of a sudden — *whomp! whomp!* — the sound of giant wings filled the air, and Gethwing landed atop the school.

Silence fell over the rooftop, first here, then there. The battle stopped.

Eric and Sparr stood side by side, breathless, swords raised at the moon dragon.

"Gethwing, leave our town alone," said Eric. "You don't belong here —"

"He doesn't belong anywhere!" snapped Sparr.

Gethwing glared fiercely at the two

boys. Then, moving his eyes from Sparr to Eric, he rose suddenly to his full height. "You, Eric Hinkle, have the Pearl Sea! Give it to me!"

Eric trembled under Gethwing's fiery gaze. The moon dragon had never seemed so huge or so cruel before. Even with the sword in his grip, even with the army behind him, his parents and his friends, Eric felt that Gethwing might actually win. "Uh, well, I . . . that is . . . no?"

"Then perish!" Gethwing roared. He raised his claws. His jaws burst with flame. Then he leaped at Eric.

Nine

Water Girl

"You stay away from my baby!" cried Mrs. Hinkle. "Come on, honey," she called to Mr. Hinkle, "that *thing* is after little Eric!"

"Little Eric?" said Sparr.

"Oh, Mom!" said Eric, blushing even as the moon dragon charged.

But his parents were fierce. Before Gethwing reached Eric, they were across the roof with twenty other parents. With rakes held high, they swatted Gethwing in mid-leap. The dragon tumbled head over heels and crashed to the roof, scattering a troop of dark knights.

"And here's a little dessert!" said Sparr, charging with his sword raised.

But Gethwing leaped up again and — *kla-bammm!* — leveled a blast at Sparr. The fiery beam glanced off Sparr's sword, but exploded near Eric and sent him reeling into Keeah. They both skittered to the edge of the roof in time to see Meredith run into the gym below, a dozen knights right on her tail.

"Keeah, we have to help her!" said Eric. As the battle resumed across the roof, he and Keeah jumped down the stairs and into the gym.

"The knights!" said Keeah. "Fire —"

"Too late!" said Eric. He rushed ahead, his sword swinging. *Fwing! Thlong!* The knights howled and fled, stumbling quickly away.

"Cool!" he said, looking his sword up and down. "This works well!"

"Nice swordplay," said Keeah, her violet sparks fading back into her fingertips.

After the knights had gone, the two friends paused and looked around the gym. It was quiet and empty. Meredith was nowhere to be seen. The next room was large and tiled and had a giant swimming pool in the middle. It, too, was empty. The cool blue water of the pool was still and unmoving.

Eric sighed. "She comes, she goes. You see her, then you don't. I almost wonder . . ."

"Yeah, me, too," said Keeah. "She seems a little, you know, magical."

The sounds of battle echoed into the room.

"They need us back," said Eric. "Who knows what my parents are up to now?"

Suddenly, ripples danced across the surface of the pool. For the next few minutes, Eric and Keeah watched the water move, as if stirred from below, until — *splash!* — the surface broke and Meredith climbed out.

"Thanks for sending those knights away," she said, shaking the water from her hair. "We weren't really getting along."

The two wizards stared at her.

"But . . . but . . ." said Eric. "You were just underwater for, like, ever!"

"I like to swim," Meredith said simply. Then she turned serious. "So, Eric, you found it, didn't you?"

He looked closely into the girl's dark eyes. "You know about the Pearl Sea? But how? And how did you know to lead me to the tree outside my house? You're, like, everywhere today!"

The girl breathed deeply. She didn't seem ruffled by Eric's questions. "I was at the coast before, too. I think I saw something I wasn't supposed to see. I saw Sparr with Gethwing."

"You saw them?" said Keeah.

The girl's face was grim. "It wasn't good."

"Tell us," said Eric.

"I'll do better than that," said Meredith. "I'll show you." Turning to the pool, she waved her hand over the water. Ripples moved across it, and the pool grew dark. A moment later, they could see shapes moving in the water.

Keeah's eyes grew wide. "How are you doing that?"

"Just watch," said the girl.

As the two friends stared down into the water, they saw Sparr and Gethwing standing alone on the rocky coast of the black sea in Calibaz.

"So, are we fooling them?" asked Gethwing, his claws raised slightly. They reminded Eric of when he made the old knights young again.

"I have their trust," said Sparr. "They think you and I are enemies. Silly, isn't it?"

"Good," the moon dragon replied. "So a new Empire of Goll will rise from the ashes of the Dark Lands. The throne of Ko will be mine."

"It will," said Sparr. "But Eric is clever. I won't find the Pearl Sea, so it must be him. But don't worry — I'll get it from him."

Staring down into the pool, Eric trembled. "I can't believe it. . . ."

Gethwing eyed Sparr. "Can I trust you to make this happen?"

The boy grinned. "Can you trust me?

They didn't call me *Lord* Sparr for nothing, you know!"

The moon dragon's eyes glowed red hot, even as he lowered his claws. Then he began to laugh. The sound of his laughter grew until the scene faded away. But before it did, Eric saw Sparr turn and touch his fins. They began to change color.

What are his fins doing? I can't see! Wait — But the scene was gone.

Eric's heart thundered in his chest. His blood raced through his veins. "I still can't believe it. Gethwing didn't have to turn Sparr. Sparr was evil the whole time! He's going to betray us. He's going to betray everyone and everything. Kid Sparr? I don't think so. He's . . . Lord Sparr again!"

"I'm only showing you what I saw," said Meredith quietly.

Keeah stared at the water for a long time. "I've seen only one person do this before. Regular people can't do that with water. They can't." She looked Meredith right in the eye. "Who are you?"

The dark-eyed girl smiled at the princess. Then, kneeling down, she drew her finger over the surface of the pool and spelled a word that remained visible in the rippling water.

M...E...R...E...D...I...T...H...

"Okay, your name," said Keeah. "But how are you doing that?"

The letters lingered for a moment, quivering on the pool's surface. Then, just before they vanished, they rearranged themselves one by one until they spelled another name.

D...E...M...I...T...H...E...R...

Keeah sank to her knees. "Oh, my gosh! Demither? Aunt Demither? You! But ... how is it possible? I mean ... *how*?"

Meredith helped the princess to her

feet. "Keeah, you freed me from Sparr's spell. You destroyed the chain that was forged the day I saved your mother —"

Eric remembered how, long ago, Sparr put Demither under a curse when she saved Relna, her sister. He also remembered the awesome moment when he joined with Keeah and Relna to free the Sea Witch from Sparr's curse.

"When that happened," the girl went on, "I fell under a spell more ancient than I knew existed. At first, I didn't know who or where I was. But somehow, like Sparr himself, I had become a child. I had no memory. I found myself here. With a different life. And still you helped me. You, Eric . . ."

When she paused, they could all hear the sounds of battle coming closer.

"How did *I* help you?" Eric asked.

"When I heard you and your friends

talking about Droon, I began to remember my past," said Meredith. "I also began to understand my mission in the Upper World."

"Your mission?" asked Eric.

The girl nodded. "I knew you had to find the Pearl Sea and that the future of Droon rests on keeping the Pearl safe."

After a moment, Keeah spoke. "Are you really free?"

The girl smiled. "I am. Thanks to you."

"Will you come back to Droon with us?" Keeah asked.

Meredith shook her head. "There are more things I have to do in this world before I come home. I can't tell you any more, yet. It may be a while before you see me again."

"But where will you go?" asked Eric. "And *how*?"

Meredith smiled. "All water connects,"

she said. "When your little pool here over-flows, it drains into pipes under the school, then into the sewers, and bit by bit into a river that winds down from the mountains to the sea. Everything connects. I'll find my way. And, Keeah, just know this. From one girl to another, I'm pretty proud of you."

With that, she dove under the water, and the surface of the pool turned spar-kling silver. When it cleared again, the girl was gone.

"I can't believe it," murmured Eric, astonished. "The Sea Witch. In my town!"

"*You* can't believe it?" said Keeah, staring into the pool. "That girl . . . was my aunt!"

The hallway erupted with the sound of clashing weapons.

"Retreat!" echoed the voice of King Zello. "We're getting whooped —"

"Come on, Eric. They need us!" said

Keeah, running out of the gym and into the hall.

But just as Eric was about to follow, something moved behind him. He whirled around, and there stood Sparr, his sword raised high.

"You!" said Eric, feeling his anger rise. "You heard that? You saw?"

"I saw," said Sparr. "So, Demither became young. Like me. That's weird —"

"What's weird is that I ever believed you!" snapped Eric. "You betrayed us. You're joining Gethwing!"

"Eric, no," said Sparr urgently, shaking his head. "Gethwing hopes I'll help him defeat Ko and raise a new empire from the ruins of the Dark Lands. A new Goll is what he wants —"

"I know what *he* wants," said Eric. "But what do *you* want?"

Sparr lowered his eyes. "I can't tell you everything yet."

"Yeah? And why not?"

"Because I don't know everything yet!" said Sparr. "I know I used to be bad. Really bad. But I'm trying to be good now. Why do you think I stopped Gethwing from questioning your mother? She might have told him something, and he would have found the Pearl Sea before you did. Can't you give me a chance? Haven't I helped you over and over again? Why don't you trust me?"

Eric wanted to believe him. He felt he *needed* to believe him. But the memory of Sparr's meeting with Gethwing was fresh in his mind. "I don't know," he said, raising and lowering his sword again and again.

Sparr smiled at the blade. "Besides, you could fight me. But you wouldn't win. I remember now what makes these swords so special. They used to belong to my mother."

"Queen Zara?" said Eric.

Sparr nodded. "She made four altogether — two for my brothers, Galen and Urik; one for me; and one for her. They were to protect us against evil magic. The blades even glow when they protect us. Except that Ko kidnapped my mother and me before she could give me mine. I was still too young. The Ancient Knights of Pim must have found them after we were taken to Droon." Sparr sighed. "Zara died before passing on everything I needed to protect myself against dark magic."

Eric looked at the blade. He knew now why he felt there was something magical about it. He also understood why Sparr had become evil when his two brothers had fought so long against it. Zara had died before she could fully protect him from it.

"Plus," said Sparr, "the sword's power wouldn't help you. It can only help —"

There was a sound in the back of the gym.

"What?" said Eric. "It can only help who?"

Hush! He's here! Sparr said silently. *Eric, my work isn't done. You have to trust me —*

What? Eric replied silently. *What do you mean?*

With a sudden thwapping of wings, Gethwing was in the room with them. "Sparr," he said, "do what you promised to do!"

At once, Sparr swiveled on his heels, blasted at the floor near Eric, then leaped, and pushed Eric down. "Give it to me. Give me the Pearl Sea!"

"What? No!" cried Eric in surprise, trying to fight back. "You're crazy. No!"

But Sparr kept him pinned down and finally ripped the Pearl from Eric's pocket. "I've got it now!" the boy yelped. Jumping up, he blasted at Eric once more and dashed out of the room, yelling, "Gethwing, come on!"

"The Pearl Sea is ours!" bellowed the moon dragon, flying after Sparr. "Knights! Follow us! The real battle can now begin!"

Instantly, the sound of knights tramping away echoed through the halls. Dumbfounded and dazed, Eric staggered to his feet. He could hear the knights running to the veil in the cafeteria.

"No . . . no . . ." he stammered. "What just happened here?"

A moment later, his friends ran into the gym.

"Eric!" said Julie, running to him.

Keeah saw Eric's ripped pocket right

away. "Oh, no! Sparr stole the Pearl Sea? He played a trick on you!"

His mind still spinning with what Sparr had said silently to him, Eric turned to Keeah. "He played a trick, all right. But I'm not sure on who!"

"We have to follow them," cried King Zello, storming in. "We have to get that Pearl back!"

"And Sparr, too!" said Eric as he jumped toward the door. "Run! Now! Everyone! Follow the knights. Follow Sparr!"

Ten

The Moon in Droon

Neal played Pikoo's horn to keep the cafeteria veil open, and everyone charged into the shadow land once more.

"Uh-oh!" cried Julie, skidding to a stop.

Everyone stopped behind her. They stared into the distance, silenced by the sight of thousands, hundreds of thousands — millions! — of dark knights moving across the scorched earth toward them.

Gethwing raised his claw, the earth

quaked, and the vast army halted. Sparr took his place next to Gethwing.

"We have the Pearl Sea," the dragon said slowly, turning to address the townspeople. "In a few moments, my Blackdark Knights will begin their real conquest of your world. Sparr and I shall return to Droon together, and that will be ours, too. I guess you could call this a bad day for you."

Eric clutched Zara's sword, not knowing what to do. Could they possibly stop the invading knights from taking over?

Gethwing turned to the boy sorcerer. "Sparr, give me the magic I seek," he said. "Then everything will be ours."

Sparr lifted his hand. The Pearl Sea sat in his palm, splattered by the rain. But he wasn't looking at it. He was staring at Eric's sword.

Eric looked down. The blade glowed ever so slightly in the dark air.

When Gethwing raised his claw toward Sparr and reached for the Pearl, Eric heard words in his head.

Blast me, Eric. Blast me, or he won't believe I'm helping him. Trust me. We can do this!

Without thinking, Eric dropped to his knees and sent a blazing silver blast right at Sparr. It struck the boy's shoulder hard.

"Ahhhhh!" Sparr screamed. His sword flashed once, then he fell to the ground, howling loudly. As he did, his hand struck the earth and — *splash!* — the Pearl dropped into a stream of rushing rainwater.

"No! No!" cried the moon dragon. He leaped into the stream, but the water seemed to clutch the tiny Pearl in its grasp and pull it swiftly under.

"My Pearl! My Pearl!" Gethwing wailed, full of rage. The moon dragon spun around at Eric. "You made this happen! You —"

Still kneeling by the stream, the dragon shouted, "Knights, attack! Attack, and take their world now!"

Thomp! Thomp! The dark troops charged toward the veils once more.

"Stop them!" cried Mr. Kroger, rushing forward with a shovel.

"Stay where you are, Dad!" shouted Neal. "I'm closing the veils!" As the knights charged, Neal put the little horn to his lips and blew into it.

Ooo-weee-ooo-weee!

The openings between the worlds vanished one by one, sealing the real world away.

Before Gethwing could open the veils again, Eric felt the sword in his hand rising higher and higher until he was holding it over his head. The blade beamed.

When its light fell over them, the warriors quivered and wobbled, they teetered and staggered, and then — *pop-pop-pop!* — the faces of every last one of them softened and wrinkled. Their shoulders slumped. Their armor lost its shine. They shrank and grew older, and their number dwindled from millions to a mere handful. Gethwing's curse was broken. They were the Ancient Knights of Pim once more.

The moon dragon uttered his dark curse again, but Eric's sword continued to shine on the knights, and they remained old.

"Ahhhhh!" roared Gethwing, pounding the black earth over and over. "Nooooo!"

"Gentlemen!" said the chief knight, sounding as he had the first time they saw him. "It's past our bedtime. Let's go back to the mountains and do what we do best — sleep!"

As the old knights mumbled in agreement, they turned away from Gethwing and stumbled slowly — very slowly! —

toward the distant hills, leaving everyone standing in the pouring rain.

Staggering finally to his feet, Gethwing turned to the children. "Next time," he snarled. "Next time, you will not win. Boy, come. We have work to do!" He pointed a claw at Sparr, who leaped onto the dragon's back, and together they swooped over to the massive pit the kids had seen from the castle's roof.

"Hurry!" cried Keeah.

The kids rushed to the pit. They watched Gethwing and Sparr dive down through the hole, and beyond it into the smoky sky over Sparr's volcano palace.

Looking back up through the pit, Sparr shot a look at Eric and spoke silently to him.

Eric, the Pearl Sea is part of the Moon Medallion. So . . . do you trust me now?

As the boy and the moon dragon

flew away into the smoky air, Eric answered him.

Yes. I do.

The kids stared down at Sparr for as long as they could. The moment he vanished into the dark sky, Eric heard a tiny *splash* from the ground. Looking down, he saw a small white stone gleaming at the bottom of the black stream at his feet.

"I can't believe it!" he gasped. He picked up the stone. It was the Pearl Sea.

"Believe that," said Keeah. "Look."

Meredith was standing far downstream. Giving them a wave, she dived into the water and was gone in a flash of silvery light.

Eric gasped. "Everything *does* connect."

"We should follow Sparr," said Julie.

"And we will!" boomed Zello from the top of the crater. "Neal, your final veil music of the day, please. Let's get everyone home!"

Neal smiled. "You got it!" As he played the strange tune once more, the king, Max, and Khan led the people back into the light of their town. At the same time, Queen Relna carefully cast a forgetting spell on all of the townspeople.

Spying his mother in the crowd, waiting to walk through the veil, Eric ran to her. "Mom. Mom! You have to tell me. Where did this pearl come from?"

Mrs. Hinkle stared at the gem, and her eyes lit up. But, almost immediately, the light began to fade. The spell was already working. "Eric," she said, "don't you remember?"

"Remember what?" he asked.

"You . . ." she said haltingly, ". . . you told me . . . you met . . . you met . . ."

"Met? Met who?"

But Relna's spell had its effect. Mrs. Hinkle forgot the experiences of the day, and so did the rest of the townspeople. She looked blankly at Eric for a moment, then headed through the veil to town.

Behind her, Eric's father blinked as he passed Zello. "I have a shirt just like that!"

One woman smiled at Khan as she went through the veil. "I want a sofa in your exact color!"

When all the people were back in town, the veil closed with a whisper, while Eric and his friends remained in Calibaz. The link between the worlds was sealed once more, and the townspeople headed off about their daily business, forgetting everything that had just happened.

"So," said Keeah, turning to her friends, "we follow Sparr and Gethwing?"

"Yeah, but I have just one question first." Eric turned to Relna. The Moon Medallion hung around the queen's neck. "It's all about this, isn't it?" he said. "Sparr said so."

Relna took the Medallion from her neck and handed it to him. Eric gently inserted the Pearl Sea into a small dimple in the center of the stone. At once, the Medallion seemed to grow around the Pearl like a frame. The shapes within the Pearl moved and swirled like waves. Then, a face appeared in the milky-white depths. It was the face of a man with a white beard.

"It's my master, Galen!" chirped Max. "Oh, it's been so long!"

The face in the stone smiled. "It has been. And now the time has come for you to find me. I'm waiting!"

The image of the wizard vanished into a storm of flakes the color of midnight.

"Black snow!" gasped Relna. "I know that place! It always snows black flakes on the far side of the moon. That's where Galen must be. That's where we must go!"

Zello laughed. "The far side of the

moon? Oh, what an adventure awaits us now!"

The children looked at one another.

Eric smiled. "Well, what else have we got to do?"

Then, leaving behind any borrowed clothes, the eight friends held hands, leaped down through the pit, and entered the dark, moonless sky over Droon.

About the Author

Tony Abbott is the author of more than sixty funny novels for young readers, including the popular *Danger Guys* books and *The Weird Zone* series, as well as *Kringle*, his hardcover novel from Scholastic Press. Since childhood he has been drawn to stories that challenge the imagination, and, like Eric, Julie, and Neal, he often dreamed of finding doors that open to other worlds. Now that he is older — though not quite as old as Galen Longbeard — he believes he may have found some of those doors. They are called books. Tony Abbott was born in Ohio and now lives with his wife and two daughters in Connecticut.

For more information about Tony Abbott and the continuing saga of Droon, visit www.tonyabbottbooks.com.

THE SECRETS OF DROON

By Tony Abbott

Under the stairs, a magical world awaits you!

❏ 0-590-10839-5	#1: The Hidden Stairs and the Magic Carpet	
❏ 0-590-10841-7	#2: Journey to the Volcano Palace	
❏ 0-590-10840-9	#3: The Mysterious Island	
❏ 0-590-10842-5	#4: City in the Clouds	
❏ 0-590-10843-3	#5: The Great Ice Battle	
❏ 0-590-10844-1	#6: The Sleeping Giant of Goll	
❏ 0-439-18297-2	#7: Into the Land of the Lost	
❏ 0-439-18298-0	#8: The Golden Wasp	
❏ 0-439-20772-X	#9: The Tower of the Elf King	
❏ 0-439-20784-3	#10: Quest for the Queen	
❏ 0-439-20785-1	#11: The Hawk Bandits of Tarkoom	
❏ 0-439-20786-X	#12: Under the Serpent Sea	
❏ 0-439-30606-X	#13: The Mask of Maliban	
❏ 0-439-30607-8	#14: Voyage of the *Jaffa Wind*	
❏ 0-439-30608-6	#15: The Moon Scroll	
❏ 0-439-30609-4	#16: The Knights of Silversnow	
❏ 0-439-42078-4	#17: Dream Thief	
❏ 0-439-42079-2	#18: Search for the Dragon Ship	
❏ 0-439-42080-6	#19: The Coiled Viper	
❏ 0-439-56040-3	#20: In the Ice Caves of Krog	
❏ 0-439-56043-8	#21: Flight of the Genie	
❏ 0-439-56048-9	#22: The Isle of Mists	
❏ 0-439-66157-9	#23: The Fortress of the Treasure Queen	
❏ 0-439-66158-7	#24: The Race to Doobesh	
❏ 0-439-67173-6	#25: The Riddle of Zorfendorf Castle	
❏ 0-439-67174-4	#26: The Moon Dragon	
❏ 0-439-42077-6	Special Edition #1: The Magic Escapes	$5.99
❏ 0-439-56049-7	Special Edition #2: Wizard or Witch?	$5.99
❏ 0-439-67177-9	Special Edition #3: Voyagers of the Silver Sand	$5.99

$3.99 each!

Available Wherever You Buy Books or Use This Order Form

Scholastic Inc., P.O. Box 7502, Jefferson City, MO 65102

Please send me the books I have checked above. I am enclosing $_____ (please add $2.00 to cover shipping and handling). Send check or money order—no cash or C.O.D.s please.

Name_____ Birth date_____

Address_____

City_____ State/Zip_____

Please allow four to six weeks for delivery. Offer good in U.S.A. only. Sorry, mail orders are not available to residents of Canada. Prices subject to change.

scholastic.com/droon 📖 **SCHOLASTIC**

If Your Dog Could Talk, What Would He Tell You?

TAYLOR-MADE TALES

THE DOG'S SECRET

by ELLEN MILES

SCHOLASTIC

New teacher Mr. Taylor can make up a great story using any five things his students choose. Give him a dog, a boat, a tennis ball, a playing card, and a necklace, and Mr. Taylor tells an exciting tale of a young girl who teaches her dog to talk and of the adventures they share.